CHINQUAPIN ROAD

BY

BONNIE N. TURNER

Table of Contents

Chapter One
March 22nd,1865

All stories must start with chapter one, but Josh Sutton's diverse chapters, however, seem scattered about much like drawings of leaves smattering on an artist's canvas, images of a breezy fall day. Such blustery squalls of dark and light, like ghostly images being seen on October's Ides, many shades of colored leaves falling in no order, but it takes them all to make the story complete.

It is out of self-preservation that Josh remembers only the wonderful chapters, carefully selected from his troubled mind until he can emotionally handle the unimaginable pain that lives in his nightmares of the others. Yes, the missing chapters are there, but over the years, he is trying to repress them, fearing they may take over his entire life if the memories are left unchecked, so maybe it is time for him to just write them down and at last purge himself of the plight of these painful memories forever. For the sake of his grandchildren, he needed to explain what had happened to him long ago.

So here is his story, which started when he was fifteen, in a time of a cruelly devastating state of war, pitting man against his brother, as morals and principles were being sacrificed in favor of survival. A time when honor was lost among deserters on both sides, as the total value of a boy's life was diminished out of desperation, it being nowhere near the value of a good mule.

Joshua Walter Sutton, born on a farm in Patrick County, Virginia, on March 22nd, 1850, was one of four children, him being the firstborn of Lawrence and Gaynelle Sutton. Born the mirror image of his mother with black hair and stark green eyes is evidence of his dark Irish ancestry. They proudly christened him Joshua Walter Sutton as a beaming father, Lee Sutton, swore Josh would do great things with his life, as he looked on in awe of what he and his beloved wife had created.

So, from the very start, Josh was under extreme pressure to be an example of perfection, setting the boy up from the start for utter failure. To put a boy or any child under such pressure was common at that time, for much was expected of the firstborn in any family. Josh never disappointed his parents as he strived to make his life beyond reproach.

The family farm was on the southwest side of the county, split apart by the Little Dan River and bordering Stokes County, North Carolina. A thriving cattle farm; also growing a cash crop of tobacco and corn. The variation ensured success in all years, be it famine or blight. No one expected the damn war that would tear the country apart; as the Sutton's lived in isolation, they never knew the severity of what was going on so far away.

Lee Sutton never believed in the concept of enslaved people or holding anyone against their will, so he never had the urge to fight for the south. They had farmhands loyal until the war started, as they were all drafted into service. The military establishment passed Lee over, dismissing him from service, for he had lost an eye to a rank bull when he was but a young man.

"It makes him look more distinguished," Gaynelle insisted as Josh always teased his mama, telling her the patch attracted her to daddy. Lee Sutton was not only handsome, but he had the gentle character rarely seen in any man. So, the pairing of Gaynelle McKensy and Lee Sutton was inevitable, for God must have smiled upon them and had deemed it so.

The road to the Sutton farm was winding into the valley, past the pine log tobacco barns, sandy bottoms of tobacco and corn, across the river, and up a hillside where the colonial home set majestically on a mound. Sugar maples lined the front yard, which meant syrup in the spring cooking, but the juice cooker produced sorghum molasses in the fall, another cash crop from the sugar cane they raised. Not one season or an acre of this farmland went to waste until the war had changed all that.

Using everything God graciously gave them, but the most beautiful of growing gifts, was the entire road was lined in Chinquapin trees. Once you cross the shallow river up the hill, they cover the road bank on the river's side, so Josh would spend all his free time happily gathering those nuts in September.

After the day's work was done, the family would gather around the fireplace at night, and daddy would read the bible or the few books they owned, as they indulged in as many chinquapins as bellies would hold. Even in wartime, they never went hungry, nor did they fear the war ever touching their valley, for surely the fighting armies would follow the main roads, not venturing into the countryside.

The most prized possession of Lee Sutton was his stallion, Gray Stone, a much-beloved horse; Lee planned on a horse farm after the war; with Gray Stone's linage, the quality of the horses would be worth the investment he had in the stallion and two mares he had bought at auction. Lee stopped riding the horses after the war started, fearing they would be noticed by loyal town folk, then the animals would be confiscated; drafted into service for the south. So, they were hiding the stallion, with a large gray mule, two bred mares, and two milk cows in the upper pasture adjoining the old cattle barn. Lee left the old draft horse in plain sight to explain how he got his fields plowed. They probably would not take the only animal he needed to feed his family.

By 1865 Josh had three sisters, Dovey, nine, Rebecca is seven; Willa is the baby, at five years old. All the girls are blonde-haired, blue-eyed, like their father. Then, as the family waited for more babies, nothing happened; whether it was the stress of war and worry, it was like mama just stopped having babies one day. It seemed Josh would be the only male among all those sisters; that was okay with him, for he could survive just fine being the one male for all his sisters to look up to. So at a young age, he declared himself an example of a gentleman, so when it came time for his sisters to choose a man to marry, they would know to look for qualities that he had shown them. This was not a hard job for Josh; he followed his father's example.

At fifteen, Josh Sutton perceived himself as a grown man, for with all the field hands gone, leaving Josh and his daddy to work hard to keep everything going. Every day was solid work, but he never complained, for many of his friends had lost their fathers in battle. It would have seemed selfish of him to say one disparaging word about the nights he was exhausted, for still having the family intact was a gift, as war seemed so far away.

The day his young life changed forever, Josh was up in the loft, throwing down the hay to the animals below. He daydreams of the war and wonders how men could go into battle to their deaths on such a glorious day. He is sweating from the heat accumulating in the loft as the sun hits the east-facing barn roof at a direct angle this morning, much like any other early spring day, but today was the only one of its kind; it is his fifteenth birthday. It made him shiver, for what if the war was still raging next year? They would probably draft him. He couldn't imagine killing another man or even a boy his age; it all seemed so surreal as he hurried to finish, trying to clear his mind of such morbid things.

Worry was a waste of energy, as he needed all he had today. It is his birthday. Mama would figure out some way to bake him a cake, even if she used molasses to sweeten it, for sugar was a luxury item now, not one they could afford, so the anticipation for his birthday celebration was on his mind as he worked.

The wool coat Josh wore was too warm, but he didn't stop to remove it as he was hurrying to finish the morning feeding. He may turn fifteen today, but years of hard labor had turned his body into a man's as he filled out his father's old coat the same as if he was twenty. The only thought he had at the moment was mama would have breakfast ready, as he could taste the hot biscuits with fresh melted butter, skillfully stirred into sugary molasses already.

He sees the bare floor of the loft and wishes for an early spring this year because the hay storage was almost gone. Last year there was a drought, so the hayfields didn't produce as much, but they always accepted that as God's will and worked with it. Strong faith had gotten them through it, as they still believed in giving thanks, for the family was together and healthy. So after a long winter and keeping these animals hidden, they needed hay to feed them. To turn them out to pasture was a sure way to get them stolen. Below him in the stables are three horses, a mule, and two cows. Daddy had let the cow herd dwindle down, selling it off, for with no farmhands and none had money to buy milk, nor beef, he decided the cows were not worth the risk of bringing thieves into the valley.

The family had hunkered down to wait out the south's resistance. Daddy had assured them, "the south couldn't last much longer at the rate the battles were being lost." Lee did not mean to sound treasonous; it was common sense to determine how it would end.

The open window allowed Joshua to see his home as he watched mama and the girls hanging out clothes on the lines. Rebecca had awakened him earlier by gobbing a piece of slimy butter into his nose before running, giggling from his room. He had responded less than gentlemanly by throwing his shoe at her.

The shoe bounced off the door as she slammed it while calling back to him, "You will have to get up earlier in the morning if you plan on being faster than me, Joshy."

"Elizabeth, stop pestering your brother. For God's sake, I don't see how he stands your constant picking." Mama called out from the kitchen below. "Use your energy to draw and heat the wash water, girl; you know today is washday. Just wish your brother a happy birthday and tell him you are sorry for being an annoying pest. Remember, young lady, you too have a birthday coming next month, so if you don't want the same treatment as him, ask for forgiveness."

Elizabeth pushed the door back open, and as she stood there, Josh was sorry he had thrown that shoe. His sister will someday be a great beauty. All his sisters looked like angels as far as he was concerned, but he knew better. She will need to work on her personality if she is ever to land a husband who can stand her.

As she smiled her most mischievous smile while sticking out her tongue, before calling out loudly, just for mama to hear, "I'm sorry brother, happy birthday."

Josh knew that was as close as he would ever get to an apology from his sister; he just rolled over and napped an extra fifteen minutes. He suddenly is awakened by the smell of biscuits baking; knowing he didn't eat until the animals did, he ran up to the barn to get the chores done. The crisp feeling in the air just told him it would be a special day.

As the horses were eating so peacefully that morning, Josh saw something crouching in the corner of the storage room. He noticed a moving shadow through the spaces in the floor planks as he looked into the storage room below. Josh figured Elizabeth was up to her usual tricks, looking outside again to see her helping mama hang clothes. So maybe it is a dog that had made its way in here as he climbed down from the loft to check on the culprit, for a stray may tend to chew on daddy's fancy leather saddle if he was hungry enough.

Josh knew of the importance of that saddle to his daddy, for it was the only thing Lee owned that had been his father's, Major Sutton. To say it was invaluable to his father was an understatement. It had been mended, the leathers redone, but the spirit was still there inside the foundation of the saddle frame.

Straight down the ladder from the loft, he stopped long enough to arm himself as he picked up the pitchfork. Then Josh headed in the direction from where he saw a shadow moving. Hating the thought of stabbing anything, but if it was a stray, it might be rabid and crazed if cornered; so many things went through his mind, but it never occurred to him to run. He had encountered nothing he feared in his fifteen years, until that day.

Gaynelle was pacing the floor nervously when her husband came in from early morning plowing. "Lee, I've rung the dinner bell for Josh to come home to breakfast for an hour now, and he hasn't returned from feeding the cows and horses. You know it is not like him to be late for a meal. Would you go up to the barn and check on him? He may have fallen out of the loft." The worry was plainly there in the deepened lines of Gaynelle's face as she looked out to the north, where the hay barn hides in the trees.

Lee kissed Gaynelle on the forehead. "I wondered why you kept ringing that bell; that is why I came home early from the field. I'll go see what his problem is; it is so unlike him to ignore you. Probably just daydreaming somewhere, I am sure. After all, it is his birthday." He was quickly heading up to the barn to see what was happening.

To be a teen boy, Josh had never caused him a day's worry or changed his daily routine a minute, so to hear that he was late coming back from feeding caused Lee concern. The ladder to the loft was straight up a wall, and there was always a chance you may misstep, but he cleared his mind to that possibility. Josh was born with the wisdom of an old man, cautious and caring to a fault. No, there was some other explanation for him being late.

Lee entered the barn, searching each room, seeing the newly dropped hay was there, largely untouched; his heart sank, the horses and mule were gone. His anxiety grew upon seeing one cow had been slaughtered inside the stall; a hindquarter was missing, looking like it was hurriedly chopped off with an ax. All the lead ropes were gone, so he quickly assumed the beef was tied to the mule, as maybe his son was tied up too. There was blood everywhere; Josh was gone, so how would Lee know it was blood from a cow or his son?

So as Lee stood there wishing he could go back to bed and this would be just a bad dream, Gaynelle walked in behind him, witnessing the slaughter; she sank to her knees; her screams could be heard across the valley until they stopped as suddenly as they started. Lee lifted her up, holding to her shaking body tightly as he spoke assuredly, stroking her black hair. "It is cow blood, Nell. Be strong, for the girls must not see this. Please trust me."

Gaynelle nodded her head up and down as she stood on her own while looking again at the cow lying in the hay. It needed to be gutted and dressed, and it was totally up to her to do that, for she was raised to be strong. Determined to not upset her husband nor the children, she became strangely calm before she declared. "I'll finish butchering the cow and salt it down the best I can, so maybe it is not wasted; Lee, grab the rifle and go after Josh now. Bring our son home."

Lee held her for a moment and whispered to her, "Take care of my babies while I am gone, Nell; I love you so. If they took the river bed, I don't know if I can track them, so just pray for us all."

"I love you, Lee; don't you dare bring me any bad news back here? Josh is as smart and stubborn as you; he will come home someday." She looked at the pitchfork and saw the blood on the prongs; she didn't have time for her imagination to get the best of her, for she had a dead cow to be gutted before it spoiled. It had warmed up very little, so maybe she could save this much-needed beef.

Lee ran to the house, grabbing a coat and his rifle, before hurrying to the bottom field where he had been turning ground for the spring cold crop plantings. He quickly unhooked the singletree and harnesses until all he had left on the draft horse now was reins that were too long to be anything but in the way. Lee promptly cut those with his knife, tying them together before pulling himself up on the giant horse's back. He didn't have time to go for the old giant's special saddle; up at the barn for every second was important in trailing whoever took his son.

Kate was big and bulky, not built for speed, but endurance, and Lee understood that as they headed toward the river, knowing that is the way he would have gone if it were him. Lee tried to think like a fugitive, figuring they would stay in the river bed to cover their tracks for several miles southeast until they assumed it was safe to go across the land. The kidnappers didn't figure in the father's determination for his son, as soon, they would realize what a mistake they had made in underestimating the love of family embedded into the boy.

Chapter Two

The Journey South

Josh had gone after what he thought was a stray dog in the cow stall, but what he interrupted was the four men who had killed old Bessie, a sweet old milk cow, then had gone about chopping off her back leg with an ax, her swelled udder still attached. They had already tied the bleeding hindquarter to Bell, the mule. The pitchfork in his hand was no match for the pistols and Sharps rifles in theirs, but he stood his ground with it, anyway.

Nervously he was thinking of his sisters and mama as he spoke, "Just take the mule with the beef and leave; there need not be any trouble. I'll even let you get a head start before telling all the menfolk in the house. I'll not begrudge a man food if he is starving; things would have been different if you had just asked."

"You talk awfully big for just a boy, don't you? If you were old enough, you would be drafted by now, so what are you, fourteen? I must say you are a big one for a fourteen-year-old; you may just come in handy along our journey south. There is one man; he is plowing the lower fields, so we will make our demands now, for we saw the woman and young girls hanging out clothes earlier. So, if you want us to stay up here and leave your sweet little sisters alone, just help us tie these animals together so we can lead them out of here quietly." The other three men just stood there staring at him, nervously holding the guns in his direction. Josh decided to take them as far from his family as he could.

The taller of the men spoke softly, "saddle up that gray stallion, for we require a new fresh mount. You will come with us as insurance; we will let you go when we are safe. Just act like you got some common sense, and you will be fine, boy. Your little sisters and mama will never see us if you use your brain." The man leered menacingly at him; the insinuation of harm to his sisters was there in the veiled threat.

Josh saddled Gray Stone as the others put leads on the two pregnant mares. Cliff Johnson eyed the boy hatefully, not at all happy to have to babysit a kid when they should be running for their lives. "Boy, you will ride the mule, so you will oversee protecting the only food we are taking with us. Lose it, and we might just skin and eat you instead." The crazed look in the man's eyes told Josh that he was foolish enough to do just that, so the boy decided, 'do whatever it takes to lead these men away from my family, away from here.'

They all saddled up as Josh grabbed the saddle horn and swung onto Bell, the mule. As Troy Brown called back to him, "boy, lead us to the river on the other side of the hill. I'm betting you know exactly how to get there without us having to pass your daddy in the field plowing. That would be a shame not having a daddy to come back home to. Besides, with daddy gone, we may just decide to spend the night here."

Josh was leading this gang of four thieves or worse, he figured them to be

Rebel deserters, for they had on some pieces of the gray uniforms, up behind the barn and over the hill, on out of sight of his home. Feeling as if he would never return, all he saw of his home place was the tops of the Chinquapin trees lining the river. Josh tried to be brave, but the tears gave his broken heart away. He wiped them off with the sleeve of the wool coat. Father's coat still had his smell embedded in the wool. That familiar smell of home will keep him sane, for he will be forever changed before this ordeal is over.

Josh made his way to the fork of the creek that ran into the Little Dan River behind the hill. Everything Josh loved had disappeared as the group galloped off, hiding their trail in the waterbed. Feeling the wetness of his tears but assuring himself the family was safe now, none of the girls were hurt, and mama was okay. They still have the draft horse, so they will be fine until he can bring the mule and the stallion home. The mares can be sacrificed. Just like that, the value of everything was quickly assessed, and the boy was forced to think like a man. He will never have the sweet luxury of thinking like a child again.

He quickly learned their names; the tall ugly one was Travis Holloway, the short one was Ed Bennett, the next was the one who worried him the most, Cliff Johnston, and then the unusual one, the scary crazy albino, was Troy Brown.

As they followed the Little Dan River into Carolina, Josh would move close to the trees, breaking a branch every chance he got, for he knew his daddy was following him. The tree branches he broke for the following days were many, and even when he knew the trail was long lost, the breaking of tree branches was the only thing that kept his young mind from being long gone as well.

About four miles down the river was a rocky road that forded the tributary, so they took it; mixing in with all the other fresh tracks there. As the three of them rode east, Ed and Josh headed west, agreeing to split and meet up in a few miles when they found a place to leave the road. That would fool anyone looking for a large traveling party with horses and one mule. They didn't think about the slow drip of blood as the cow's leg was bleeding out.

Soon the party was following the Dan River onward east as Travis called back to Troy, "We will camp outside off Leaksville tonight and try to steal some more clothes if we can. That is your job, Troy. This time try to find shoes big enough to fit me. My toes are cramped and raw; you know how miserable that can be. Stay out of sight, for we don't need a bunch of townfolks hunting us down thinking there will be a reward."

"I'll try, but the odds of finding shoes for your feet are not that good," Troy smirkingly answered while glaring at the shoes Josh had on. They were well worn but looked to be his size, so he would just take those in the morning. He didn't figure the boy would put much of a fight, and if he did, well, he had an excuse to kill him.

Josh felt Troy staring at him, and it made his skin crawl; he urged Bell on forward to put Edd Bennett between them.

Lee Sutton was about five miles away from his boy as the sun was setting, and the moon wasn't full enough tonight to follow an already lost trail. He had lost them once they left the river and split up. Lee had followed the drops of blood, but eventually, those even stopped as the party crossed fields where the grass and underbrush soon absorbed them like any phantom in the darkness of night.

Lee knew all hope of following them was lost, as the hardest decision he would ever make was now knowing he would return home tomorrow to protect the rest of his family. They had raised that boy right; Josh had acute judgment. So as Lee prayed to God while lying there, unable to sleep, he was thinking of the pressure he had always put on Josh to be an honest Christian man. Now, the boy is traveling in the company of horse thieves, and worse, how was Josh, being so kindhearted, going to survive? As a father, is he doing the right thing, was heading back home a wise decision? Lee prayed it was for the best; he must consider his girls alone and defenseless as that gave him no choice.

This time, Lee started back to Virginia on well-traveled roads, heading west, stopping in Walnut Cove to report the kidnapping to the Stokes County Sheriff's office. They dispatched telegrams statewide and into Virginia with a description of Josh, the horses, and the mule, for no one really knew who took him. By then, the kidnappers were long out of Stokes County's jurisdiction, so Lee headed home with a heavy heart and little hope of help from law enforcement, for there was a war going on, as the morals of men had gone to hell.

Gaynelle ran out to greet him as soon as she first heard hoofbeats on the road. She had been sitting on the front porch swing watching the road as the sun was setting when she saw him returning home, alone. Running to greet him, she fell into his arms, then as he held her tight, he sobbed in his grief, for he had failed her. Wiping away the tears, she said, "Come inside and eat. You did everything you could do; the girls and I need you. Joshua will escape and make it home; I know this as sure as I know there is a God. We will set the table for him every night until his return, even if it takes forever. Our boy will come home to us."

It was a somber homecoming for the girls, who would sadly look at their father across the dinner table and burst into tears, unable to eat, for they wondered if their brother was eating tonight. "Who took him, papa, and why him?" Willa, the youngest, was having the most challenging time of the three. "Will they want me next? We are all just little and not of much use to anyone." She looked up at her father and declared, "I hate the Rebels, and if I marry, it will be a damned Yankee."

What could a father say? His baby girl earned the right to curse. "Knowing your brother's heart, he would have led them away from you. He has always been so protective of you girls. Willa, it will be a long time before you have to worry about a husband, and by then, all this separatism will hopefully be a thing of the past."

"But papa, who is protecting him? What if he is cold and hungry, or if they hurt him? What if he is dead already? Why would they need to keep him alive?" Elizabeth started to cry. "I was always annoying him. I am so sorry."

The table fell silent until Gaynelle spoke up quickly. "God is watching him, so let us do an extra prayer every night until Josh is back home with us. Wherever he might be, he may hear it, and it will give him the strength to make it home to us."

"Will he be home by the time the chinquapins are ripe? You know how much he loves to gather them." Dovey asked. "If he isn't back by then, we will pick them and save them for when he returns."

"Silly, they haven't bloomed yet," Rebecca broke in quickly, seeing she had hurt Dovey's feelings; her attitude changed to trying to be kind, "But then who am I to say when the trees will bloom? If he does not come home, I hope the trees never bloom again," Rebecca had cried as they all finished the meal in silence. The family core had been shattered, and for the first time in his life, Lee Sutton felt helpless. He didn't even know what to say to his daughters to calm their fears.

Days away from home, he heard his captors say they camped near Kinston, North Carolina, last night. Now, Josh wondered how long he could remain calm and not let Cliff Johnston get under his skin. The man was vile, cursing with every word and leering at him like he smelled a freshly baked apple cake. Cliff was the more handsome of the four, but he was also the one Josh feared the most. Something about him was just not right to Josh, not that anyone who would kidnap a child was normal. The man just made his flesh crawl like he was soulless and evil.

Josh tried to ride as close to Ed Bennett as possible, for Ed was a Christian man reading the bible as they rode along. Indeed, anyone who needs to read the bible that much would protect him from the likes of Cliff, but then he seemed right at home with the devil, so maybe he wasn't anything but a fraud.

"Mr. Bennett, how long have you been with these men? It seems odd you would be comfortable in their company when you appear to be a good, God-fearing Christian.”

Ed turned to look at the child who was openly judging him, and for a moment, he knew the boy was in the right to ask the question. “You will learn, boy, someday that you pick the devils you travel with during wartime. You must dance with the one who brings you. When they escaped, these men brought me with them; I, too, was a captor for a few weeks, until I realized they were looking out for me. You will come to that conclusion soon. I am heading home to Savannah, and to do that, I’ll ride with the devil himself. I just want to see my wife and baby girl again. They have not forgotten me and I need to know that.

Josh looked shocked at the man, desperate to see his child, as he just blurted out, “How can I pity you not seeing your wife and child when my mama wants her son back? She wants to see me back safely in my bed. Do you even realize you are like them? You are hypocritical preaching so vociferously to the Lord when you are nothing but a child kidnapper and horse thief just as much as the other three." He looked hatefully at the man before drifting away from Ed Bennett for the worst thing in the world his daddy always said was a hypocrite.

Before dark, they stopped at a riverbank to cook more of the rotting cow's thigh. Josh gathered wood and started the campfire as the four men had already made pillows of the saddles and blankets and lazily watched. He assumed he was the slave now as he cut thick pieces of the cow and skewered them on a stick, cooking them as the four men dozed.

The smell that arose from the meat heating was so bad that Josh had to run to a nearby bush to throw up anything in his already empty belly. Josh had not eaten beef since yesterday, preferring the wild greens he gathered in the lowlands as they set up camp. Troy Brown had laughed at him, but Josh knew the dangers of eating rotten anything. These men, however, had starved for so long they didn't realize how nasty the beef had become. Then again, Josh saw the maggots embedded in the meat as he cut it to cook. The trick was to not over-cook to give them a good dose of the old belly gripes. If they were sick, heaving, he might be able to get away.

The rotten smell made Josh heave as he took each man a speared stick with thick chunks of gray beef, hot grease dripping as they all dug in and ate every piece. Josh was still gathering wild watercress, and although they thought he had eaten the cooked meat, he just fixed his own bed as he lay there and waited.

Eventually, these men were going to be so sick they would not even notice when he stole their guns to take a chance to escape. He was not going anywhere without the guns, the horses, and the mule they stole.

Every day since they left the farm, Josh had tried to keep his bearings as to the direction they were heading in. It appears they are heading southeast as the sun rose every day in the order. They headed off in that direction. So, he needed to return northwest, as he wondered when the opportunity would arise for him to use his navigational knowledge.

It seemed forever since he had seen his family, and he lay there remembering he had thrown a shoe at Rebecca. God, he wished he could go back to his birthday; he would not have gotten mad at her simple prank. Rebecca loved him, and she only wanted his attention. He missed her so much, and he wished he had acted differently. He would tell her he was so sorry if he ever made it home. That all his sisters were his life. She could butter his nose every morning, and he would say nothing.

Josh waited for the men to get sick, but all that happened was lots of gas, and Ed got the runs, but no one got ill enough for him to escape. Now feeling all hope was gone as he cried himself to sleep. Josh had been brave up to that point, but what had that gotten him? He just let the heavy veil of homesickness engulf him as he tried to keep quiet, not wanting these men to see him cry.

There were many opportunities in the next few days for him to just ride off, as the men didn't seem to care anymore if he was with them or not. Even if Josh escaped, they were far enough away from Virginia that no one would care. They had more important things to concern themselves with. Josh could have just left, but he swore to go nowhere unless he had Gray Stone, the saddle, and the mule at the least to return to Daddy.

Chapter Three
Surrender

Joshua had been awake for about an hour just listening to the frogs that lined the riverbank singing their courting songs of spring. The water sounded so peaceful as he wondered if this same water had flowed through his farm a few days ago. At first light, he planned on gigging a few of those frogs for breakfast, frog legs being a delicacy he loved. Maybe if Josh caught enough, they would let him have at least one.

Since the rotten cow was at last gone, he made himself useful by securing anything he could spear to feed them all, so they realized how useful he was to keep around. His one fear was that they would just cast him out now, meaning he could never return the animals home.

Then he started hearing the soft whinnying of Gray Stone, the recognizable sounds the stallion always made when someone came near him. He was a natural-born beggar, loving any treat given to him. Someone was out there with his father's horse, so that could not be good, for someone was trying to steal him; whether it was one of his captors or a stranger, he couldn't let that happen.

He coughs a few times loudly until he sees Travis stirring awake. Then he saw Travis pull the Sharps rifle from under his saddle blanket. Josh just waited to see who was taking Gray Stone, braced to run and grab the horse reins before the inevitable shot would scare the animal off.

Travis was awakened by Joshua's coughing, then the sound of the horses nickering as if someone were with them. He pulled his rifle from under his saddle blanket. Making his way through the misty fog of morning light, he could make out the shadow of someone saddling the stallion he had claimed early on as his. It was Troy Brown who had just swung himself on the top of the saddle; the morning was silent until the gunshot rang out. He slumped and fell with a thud to the ground.

Josh scrutinized all of this as his first thought was the horse as he ran to catch

Gray Stone before the startled stallion ran off, getting lost for good. He wished he felt a single shred of pity for the dead man, but his singular purpose was to return his family's property to Chinquapin Road. None of these raiders will stop him from that, being it is the only thing of importance in his life now. It was the first dead man he had ever seen, and amazingly, he felt nothing.

Josh was thinking of home, so homesick, as it brought a tear to his eye, which Travis noticed as he pulled Tony Brown toward the river, then rolled him into the swift-moving waters. Josh stood there silently praying, "Thank you, God. One down and three to go. Amen"

Travis looked in amazement; why would this boy care enough to pray for his kidnappers? He turned to leave, mumbling in a low, warning voice. "Have no pity for him, for I have witnessed his deeds before. Save your prayers for the deserving."

Josh considered it rude to interrupt anyone in prayer or otherwise, but it did not surprise him since these men were best described as disgusting. "And sir, I just witnessed your deeds, so do I not have pity for you when someday I witness your death? Do I rejoice or pray?" Joshua was restrained from showing any more emotions because he knew it made no difference to these men, for they are fundamentally evil and beyond caring for anyone but themselves.

Josh managed to spear enough frogs for them all to have four legs each; with one gone, the math added up in his favor. Travis had made sure the boy had received a fair share at breakfast, for he knew it was Joshua who awakened him to the horse thief, so now he would be sure the boy stayed close, for he mistakenly took that betrayal of one of the others, as loyalty to him.

Like any lesson learned the hard way, Joshua now had a plan to eliminate them one at a time until he was down to one. Then it would be up to him to take care of the last one somehow. He knew the penalty of being a horse thief and a kidnapper, so he decided it was his Christian duty to declare justice for the crimes these three had done. Troy had paid his debt, so now it was three more heathens to go. Joshua figured it would be the preacher, Ed Bennett, who will be the next on Cliff's list, with his help. So, as he prayed, he directed his judgment request to the preacher in heartfelt prayer this time.

Chapter Four

The Missing Plate

"We missed Joshua's birthday, so tonight, we will pretend he is here with us, as we all pray really hard. He may just hear us wherever he is resting tonight." Dovey was looking at the meal her mother had prepared; before, she never gave much thought to where the food came from. Now, to imagine her brother out in the wilderness, maybe homesick and afraid, making just sitting and eating with family so hard some nights that she couldn't take it. Joshua was a few years older than her, and being brave was not in her nature for so much frightened her lately. Night terrors of being taken by men with faces shrouded. Did Joshua go with them to save her and her sisters? Dovey had overheard mama and daddy talking about that possibility. When he returns, she will make his days wonderful and carefree. She would always behave like the good girl she knew she could be.

Dovey silently prayed, 'God, please bring him home so I can show him how much I love him.'

They were just five miles from New Bern, North Carolina, when they decided the horses needed a good rest and some food. Travis had seen the value of the two pregnant mares and the price such fine horses would bring at a legitimate auction. Travis walked over to where Josh brushed the stallion down with care, tending to the saddle sore on Gray Stone's back. "What breed are these three?"

"Not purebreds of any type; we could never afford that."

"Don't lie to me, boy; I see the way you coddle them and tend to them like they came over on the boat from Egypt. Are they Egyptian pedigree?"

"They are Patrick County lineage, nothing special, not good to pull a plow at all."Josh stopped grooming Gray Stone and walked off, hoping Travis would just forget that conversation, for it may be in his head to sell these animals soon. No way would he ever tell him their actual value.

Ed Bennett had been scouting all morning, leaving before the others had awakened. He was supposed to be looking for pasture for the horses since sunup. Travis is now sourly watching Ed crossing the shallow stream to the campsite pulling something behind him; she was having trouble walking, causing him to be even slower than usual. "Damn that idiot, what has he done now. Dragging trouble right into our camp, probably with an irate family following him." Travis was rubbing the butt of his rifle, looking for any excuse to rid himself of the self-righteous idiot, annoyed that it always took Ed too long to get anything done, and they were in danger waiting for his slow ass to return, exposed, out in the open like this. Now he has kidnapped a girl of all the new trouble they did not need.

Ed stopped to let the girl get her footing before continuing toward them. She would stumble and cry out in pain, for he had the girl tied by the hair to the saddle horn. Now, Ed is looking at Travis worriedly, knowing he would have to answer to someone for what he had done to this young girl and her baby.

Ed rode up beside the only man on earth he truly feared as he blurted out, "The baby wouldn't stop crying, Travis. Do you hear me? It was screaming, and you know how I can't stand that. I'm shell-shot from the war but praise God, I'm a sinful man, please have mercy on me; I hit it in the head with my fist, then shook it until it stopped crying; after that, the woman stopped fighting me too. Look at the scratches on my face and bite marks on my hands. Can't you see I had no other choice? Look at her; she is an unholy temptress, a Lolita. The child, I am sure, was going to be like her and wasn't that pure either. If both were just sent on to their just reward, I'd be called a servant of God forever."

Ed Bennett had bound the young girl by the hair; strands of it had pulled out, now entangled in the rope he used to secure

44

her to his saddle horn. She barely had enough slack to stand, must less keep up with the horse. Her scalp was bleeding, the blood running onto her eyes. Even so, the girl wasn't screaming or fighting to get free. She had become quietly submissive. Ed had her bloody undergarments tied around her face, shoved into her mouth, using them to gag her so she couldn't scream. The woman's face was bruised, horribly beaten; her dress was ripped to shreds. Her dark red hair was matted with blood; as she struggled not to fall, for Ed had her wrists bound behind her as she was forced to walk beside the horse.

"She said we couldn't use her pastures for a few days; she needed all that grass for her goats, a tiny condescending thing she was, and I'm afraid I lost my temper. I said we need that grass for our starving horses, and she slammed the door in my face." Ed was sniffling in his guilt and shame and was trying to justify what he had done to the one person he feared, Travis, but Travis didn't like what he saw. Ed had wasted their time indulging in his own lustful desires while they waited on him like a bunch of fools. He was sent out to scout not to rape and potentially murder a child.

"Looks to me like she made you lose your religion too there, Ed. Surely you, of all people, didn't kill her baby. Don't tell me that is what you are saying; is that what I am hearing, Ed?" Travis was choking up while staring at the milk-stained circles on the woman's dress as the milk was flowing for a child that would never need it again. Travis was a killer, but he had standards as far as a mother and child were concerned. At least he had once upon a time, but to look upon the girl's face, no wonder Ed lost his religion. She was an angel, but like Ed said, all sinners must repent, and judgment day was here, for this was more trouble than Travis had time for. It was not how he planned his morning to go, but it seemed the order was sent down from above as divine guidance moved his hand to his gun.

Travis quickly pulled his pistol and aimed it at the girl, who just stood there, broken and not flinching but waiting for this nightmare to end. "So, girl, you denied us use of your pastures and planned on keeping the grass for damn goats while we have starving horses here. What the hell has happened to hospitality and sharing of your bread. Are you a Christian girl? Where is the father of the baby, or do you even know? We would have paid you for the grass. Then you tempted this Godly man with your soiled body; what a harlot you are."

"That is right, Travis; rid us now of this devil spawned sinful temptation. Hallelujah," Ed called out, triumph in his voice as he assumed they forgave him and the need to answer his sins would be gone. "She did this to me; she invaded my mind with sinful thoughts."

Travis drifted the gun in Ed's direction, and before Ed could open his mouth to explain, Travis shot him in the forehead. "Repent, yeah, sinner, repent," Travis mockingly laughed. "I guess we will not be under his judgemental eye anymore, for hell is his just reward. A child killer is just more than I can stand to look at day after day. He rests in peace and has gone home to be with the Lord, for he was assured he could do no wrong as long as he held onto that bible. Well, I hoped it worked for him, but I imagine hell just got hotter. ”

Josh realized the danger at once as he ran out to catch the startled horse, for the woman was tied by the hair to the saddle, and if the horse ran, it would drag her to her death. Quickly taking off his coat, covering the half-naked woman, he saw how young she was, hell not much older than him; as their eyes met, he sensed her shame and hopelessness.

Eye contact between them for just a moment, but Travis interrupted as he called out. “Girly, just escort us back up to your cabin, and we will see your baby gets a proper burial. We will stay there for a few days to let the horses feed and rest. We have pushed them hard for days now, and we all will need to rest and have a good home-cooked meal. We can save our introductions for later, as we will all remember to be more mannerly than our late friend here. I’m afraid he let a pretty face turn his head and other things.” Travis was staring at the girl, and his entire persona seemed to change. “I’m

guessing your face was pretty before Ed
so savagely beat you." Travis' eyes
stalked the girl's body as he continued his
shameful gaze. He regained composure
and threw a pocketknife to Josh. "you
untangle her hair, cut it from that rope,
and set her free. She will not be running
away or fighting us anymore. Looks like all
the fight has been beaten out of her and
what she was fighting for, well, is
probably dead." Travis spits toward the
dead man, lying face down in the mud.
"He has been a hindrance ever since we
left. I'll surely not miss him or his bible-
thumping lies. How about you, Josh? Will
you miss this self-proclaimed, hypocritical
devil? I believe you saw through him long
before we did." Travis looked at the young
boy, who was probably more man than
them all put together, deciding he would
no longer hold him here. He would release
the boy in a few days, with that mule he
seems so attached to. The boy had
caused them no harm and had been
helpful for the last few weeks. Josh could
try to make his way back home, and
someday, he may look back on this time

as an adventure. A break from a life of boredom.

Josh didn't speak but casually slipped the pocketknife in his jacket, thinking, 'two down, two to go.' Travis didn't even realize Josh had kept the knife, for he was busy thinking about the girl now.

Josh removed the girl's gag and then carefully untangled her long hair from the rope that held her tightly to the saddle. He saw no reason to cut her beautiful hair. She had endured enough insults. "Just keep that coat to cover yourself, miss; I'll not be needing it again until next winter, anyway."

"My name is Ruth," she whispered to him. "Please check on my baby when we get to the shack. It matters not what they do to me; just help my baby, safe from them. Please, if she is beyond help, will you be merciful?" her voice caught in a sob. "Please, say a prayer as you bury her?"

"I promise I'll tend to her, mam. Don't fight them, for they will kill you. Just do what it takes for you to live. I am not here of my free will, so just do whatever it takes to stay alive."

"What are you two whispering about? Don't be muttering behind my back, or I'll quickly rid myself of you both as easily as old Ed here."

"Well, let us bury him," Cliff spoke up. He had been worriedly watching how Travis was eyeing the girl. A female can make even the kindest soul evil, and Travis's soul was already there.

"And waste a buzzard's fine meal. No, I will not bury Ed for what he had done. Cliff, is it worth us getting caught before we leave here?" Travis had gathered the horse's reins, and he was leading them across the stream, headed up the hill in the direction Ed had come from.

A few miles up the road, the girl cried louder as she ran toward her shack. Cliff galloped to stop her, but Travis called, "Let her go. It is the baby she is concerned for; she might as well find out that it is gone already for herself. Cliff, make yourself useful and butcher one of those young goats in the pasture. Looks like we will eat good tonight, and so will the horses. It has been so long since I slept in a bed and had a decent meal. Maybe we can find some of her man's clothes and take a bath. Clean clothes and a bath; who could ask for more."

Cliff rode off toward the pasture to slaughter a goat as Josh followed Travis to the corral gate. Then, leading the horses into the large barn, they unsaddled all the animals before turning them onto new grass. Josh noted a stream nearby for freshwater. "These starved animals will be fit to journey again in a few days if they don't founder themselves on new grass," Josh told Travis, seemly to be concerned about the health of his father's animals purely for the benefit of the outlaws' escape.

Travis looked at the boy who had indeed grown several inches in the last few weeks; he saw a man. That was not good for the boy would be inclined to go home, but the man may just try and kill him. No, this boy didn't have it in him; he is one of those born with goodness in their hearts. Travis laughed at that thought as he headed toward the house.

Josh noticed Travis left the rifle in the holster on the saddle he had pulled off Gray Stone. Now the promise he made of bringing the animals home was burning in his mind. It seemed an impossible mission a few days ago when there were four men to fight; that was not the case anymore as he breathed a silent prayer, "God help me do this deed, and then please forgive me. I'll never ask for anything more, but let me save Ruth and her baby."

Travis's thoughts are mostly consumed with Ruth, for he had the next few days planned; it had been years since he had slept with such a fine young woman. Once her baby was buried, he was sure she would be more hospitable toward them. First, he would have to eliminate Cliff, for he hated sharing anything.

When the men came into the house, Ruth was holding her baby, nursing the child who was drinking greedily, seeming to be unhurt, other than a large bruise on its face.

'Ed had hit the baby with his fist,' thought Josh, realizing at that moment whatever it took to protect that baby girl he would do. 'How can grown men be so evil? But then they kidnapped a child.' Funny, he considered himself a child no more since he was forced to grow up.

Cliff had brought the skinned and dressed goat into the kitchen, then was busy building a fire in the stove to cook it. Laying it on the table, he produced a bloody knife from its leather sheath and started cutting off strips of the best loin. Once, Cliff had the meat removed and the entire animal was in a large pot to boil, he threw the soup bones out of the kitchen door. He didn't figure any of them would be around long enough to need them.

Then he went to draw water to heat for a tub bath. Cliff hadn't enjoyed a tub bath in two years, and although Travis' attention was elsewhere, Cliff tried to ignore the woman, who he was sure could use a hot bath, as well. That nasty Ed had beaten her badly, now she had dried blood caked to her body. Cliff trembled in rage, for he would never have done that; he would have been gentle to her and the child, for she was too beautiful to be mutilated.

Ruth looked like his late wife, who had died in childbirth within a month of his leaving for Richmond. Cliff blamed himself for her death, for he stupidly volunteered for this senseless war; he had left her. What a fool he had been, for all he gained was the promise of the hangman's rope; payment due for being a traitor if he is caught.

Josh was making his way back to the barn, and there on the saddle was the rifle Travis had just left there in his haste to be inside the house with Ruth. Josh pulled the gun from the holster and checked to see if it was loaded. It was. He had this one chance to save the woman and the child, then, if the Lord will, make his way back home. It seemed to be someone else who walked toward the kitchen and opened the door.

Cliff was naked in the tub, taking a much-needed bath, anticipating his turn with Ruth, when the rifle rang out as the bullet entered the back of his head. He was knocked forward as the water turned red.

Josh ran to hide behind the door, as Travis came barging in naked, with a pistol, as he too received a bullet to the back of his head. Travis fell forward onto the floor; not until then did Josh let go of the grip on the trigger as he realized his ordeal was finally over. He sat down in the kitchen chair, watching the blood slowly drip from the hole in the back of Travis's skull. It was a beautiful sight. Then Josh looked at his hands, the hands of a coldblooded killer. He tried to feel remorse, but he felt nothing but pleasure as he looked up and said with joy in his heart. "Thanks be to God. I am going home."

Josh rushed in to check on Lucy, who was naked, screaming, clinging to her baby, "Please, don't kill me. My baby needs me." At that moment, Josh realized he was still clinging to the rifle, pointing it carelessly at the helpless girl, who was kneeling on the floor begging for her life.

Josh dropped the rifle and ran to cover Ruth with what was left of the dress she had been wearing. "They are both dead, Ruth. Nobody is going to hurt you anymore. Not as long as I am here anyway, for you have nothing to fear from me. Clean yourself up and tend to the baby while I use the mule to drag those bodies down to the river and dispose of them for good. Then I'll clean up the mess I made of your kitchen."

Ironically, Josh used the same ropes Travis had used to steal his father's animals to pull the kidnapper's bodies to the river; he dumped them in once there. He would probably have never killed them for the kidnapping, then them being horse thieves, but what they were doing to Ruth went against everything he had ever been taught about respect for women, for Josh could hear her begging and screams all the way out at the barn. That was the last straw, as the rifle was somehow just placed in his hands. Sometimes justice is handed out by God, and sometimes he uses the meekest of his flock to execute it.

Chapter Five
April 19ᵗʰ, 1865

After being on good pasture for a few weeks, the animals are well-fed and rested, ready to make a long journey north. It is time for Josh to start back home to Virginia; this time, his journey will serve two purposes, and he will not be alone.

Lucy's husband was killed before her baby, May was born; the home is not hers but a sharecropper's shanny. The owner had told her already she must find somewhere else to live for she would bring trouble, and Josh guessed that the man was right. He insisted Ruth conceal herself in men's clothes and a straw hat to make traveling with her more accessible.

So on that beautiful day, they started northwest with seven horses and a mule and nine goats strung out with leads; the journey was slow and hard on Ruth and May. The first town they came to, they traded Cliff's horse and the goats that were slowing them down for a buggy and enough money for provisions and grain for the animals for a month. Ruth and the baby could be more comfortable now, and in the General Mercantile, Josh had bought a map. He learned they were two-hundred and fifty miles from home, but now he had empty roads, so no more hiding in the woods. He was not so comfortable traveling the open roads, but he clung to the rifle and now wore Cliff's pistol as well.

Josh knew that his family would take Ruth in, for she was a war widow, having no one to protect her or the baby. He had no doubts about them accepting her, but he wondered how he could face his family, for he was returning home a killer. Not just of one man, but two. In the months he was gone, he had changed. Josh had no desire to see the world, for all he saw was ugly. He would be content to be a good man for the rest of his days or as good as the world let him be.

Everyone they met on the road heading south called out that the war was over. The south had lost, but there seemed to be a suggestion of pure relief that things could go back to normal and the men would be free to return home. Ruth was dressed as a man, as she would have the baby hidden under the old wool coat Josh had given her. They slept in the buggy at night, but mostly Josh set up not able to rest but just keeping guard.

After a few days, Ruth realized how exhausted he was. "You know I can drive this buggy as good as you, so get in the back and sleep. Fix a cot for you and May; I'll wake you if need be. The road is pretty straight for the next fifty miles, and I'll stop when I get tired to take a break and feed May. I'll wake you if I see trouble."

Josh looked at the girl who was not that much older than him as he asked, "How old are you, Ruth?"

"I'm sixteen."

Josh looked at her with nothing but concern; the girl who must have married when she was not much older than his sister, whom he considered still a child. "Why did you marry so young?"

"I don't ask myself why for anything anymore, for if I studied on it, I'd go crazy.

May is my responsibility now. I'll do whatever it takes to keep her safe; at least I tried."

"Did you love your husband?"

Ruth did not want to answer Josh's questions, for no, she didn't love him, she didn't hardly know him before he took off with his brothers to die. That was so long ago, it seemed, and now they needed to get the horses moving north again. "Take a nap, Josh, for you are getting too nosey in your questions, and it is really none of your business. My husband's death seems a lifetime ago, but it was only last year. He was still a kid himself and followed his brothers off to war. None of them returned, but all three died on the same day. I've made it this far, and I will continue on. I know you think your folks will take May and me in, but so far in this lifetime, I've not seen too many folks that kind." Ruth pulled herself up onto the buggy as Josh took May; they both went to rest in the back of the wagon.

It had been a few years since she had driven horses, but it was like she had remembered. They moved on at a slowed pace, for the two pregnant mares were slowing them down. They would deliver within a few weeks. Ruth just prayed they made it back to Josh's home, for she couldn't envision him with such a kind heart leaving those mares and foals behind.

Chapter Six

May 5th, 1865

They had started their journey north just two weeks ago, so this morning as Josh looks at the road that would take him back home, it is lined in Chinquapin trees in full bloom. Taking a deep breath, trying hard not to cry his tears of pure joy, he is also looking down at the back of Gray Stone and Bell as they are pulling the wagon, bringing them all home. For the last ten miles, Gray Stone hadn't needed the guidance of the reins. It was as if he knew where he was, and he, too, was going home.

Josh had promised himself to not return without the stallion and the mule; he figured the pregnant mares would never withstand the journey. He was wrong, and although they will foal any day now, the mares proved as up to the challenge as the stallion and mule. He had all-new respect for females of any kind.

The sound of the wheels on the gravel road echos into the dale as Gray Stone calls out his happiness at being back in his valley. The distinct scream of a stallion claiming his land was the sound heard at the farmhouse as Lee was sitting on the front porch with Gaynelle. They look at each other before they both run down the road toward the wagon that had just forded the river.

It was moving toward them; a wagon with three horses and a mule pulling it, and the two pregnant mares trailing behind. Josh was driving, and he had a girl with the reddest of hair sitting beside him holding an infant.

Josh didn't even stop the buggy, but handed the reins to Ruth as he jumped out and ran toward his parents. He was crying, forgetting he was now a man. He was just a boy who had been through hell, and he needed his mama. Josh ran to her, picked Gaynelle up, and held to her so tightly, burying his face in her hair as Lee's arms encircled them both.

"How are the girls?" was his first question. "Can we find room here for Ruth and her baby?" was the second.

Lee answered, his voice choking with emotion, "They have missed you so, and yes, Ruth can stay here as long as she wants to. I knew you would bring the stallion back home in my heart, but this is a little overwhelming, boy. No, I'll change that, for from now on, son, I will refer to you as a man."

Chapter Seven
March 22nd, 1868

Josh is celebrating his 18th birthday today as he is also celebrating his wedding day to Ruth. Today she will become Mrs. Josh Sutton, and May will be the flower girl and Josh's daughter.

It turned out Ruth never wanted to leave this valley at the end of Chinquapin Road, for Ruth found it was always intended to be her home. She flourished here, loving her new family as much as she loved the one who rescued her, Josh.

Lee and Gaynelle treated her like their own daughter, as they spoiled and showered May with all the love of any grandparents.

Rebecca, Dovey, and Willa all loved their new sister, and now they have a niece in May, for she was the baby they all had waited for so long. Best of all, their brother was home, and they knew it was no coincidence that he arrived in time to see the Chinquapins' blooms.

Although Josh never asked her to marry him, it was taken for granted he would, for everyone to see how he loved her and May. Even more, than he loved her, Josh respected her, so he let her choose who she wanted to spend her life with, and as destiny would have it; it turned out to be him.

Chapter Eight
March 22nd, 1950

Joshua Sutton was rocking while looking toward the river, having to imagine the trees lining the dirt road, for his eyes had failed him years ago. All he had now were vivid memories, floating like leaves into his mind, so to him, the Chinquapins are in bloom all year round. Along with his eyes, so much more God had taken from him, as he often wondered if it was because of the horrible secrets he never told his family about how he made it home. Ruth never mentioned it; she had blocked all of that time from her fragile mind, for to remember was more than a kind heart could bear. Now it is only sounds, not sights, he recognized of his farm, as he could hear horses neighing in the distance all descendants of Gray Stone. Many grandchildren playing in the yard, probably under the sugar maples.

It was his birthday. May was baking him a cake in the kitchen; he still had a keen sense of smell as he smiled, wondering how he lived one hundred years. It was certainly not a blessing in some ways, so maybe it was punishment as he watched his wife, mother, father, sisters, and five children pass away, and his sentence was he was still here.

Josh felt the child take his hand ever so gently as he helps the girl into his lap. It is Isabell, May's great-granddaughter, who was always wanting Grandpa to tell her stories. "So, my Isabell, what story do you want to hear today?" He laughed as she reached up to touch his eyes with gentle hands. "Why aren't you playing with your cousins out in the yard?"

"I would rather have you tell me one of your stories." She cuddled closer to him and said, "Please! First, I have questions."

"What questions are worrying your mind today?"

"Grandpa, why don't your eyes work anymore?" she sweetly asked with the innocence of a child.

"There are just so many things you are allowed to see in your life, both good and bad, so you see, by the time you reach my age, you will have seen them all. I don't miss seeing things so much for my sweet child; I bet you are as beautiful as your Granny Ruth. Did I ever tell you how I met your grandmother, Ruth?" He took a deep breath and smiled as he continued, "It was a lovely spring day, and it was also my birthday. I was feeding the horses and cows up in the barn when I heard a noise, so I went to see...."

Josh Sutton stopped speaking and became still, he could never tell his story; he had put it off too long. For, at that moment, his heart stopped forever as he recalled his ordeal and what he had to do to survive. Josh made a promise to his father, and he always kept his promises, for he had promised Ruth to meet her by the Little Dan River and travel up Chinquapin Road with her again someday.

Now Isabell will have to wait for another time and place to hear the story Granpa Sutton started to tell, for Josh Sutton closed his eyes, taking that sad story to his grave.

The End

About the author;

Bonnie Turner still lives in Patrick County, Virginia, and grew up on Chinquapin Road.

Thanks to the spirit of Josh for his story is finally told.

Books by Bonnie N. Turner

The Eyes of Freya

Forever Freya

Freya Lives

Freya's Army

Freya Sees Something Wicked

The Infamous Fairies of Fairystone

Ava the Dragon's Daughter

Freya; Casting the Second Stone

Freya Knows

Fae; of Ash and Wood

All the Pretty Wildflowers

Tomilyn's Revenge

Willowdean

Degrees of Separation;

Draykerr's Daughter

Lost

Bonnie Blue

The Whip-poor-will Sings

Paradise Plantation

www.ingramcontent.com/pod-product-compliance
Lightning Source LLC
Chambersburg PA
CBHW072038150726
47999CB00002B/974